VANSHIKA

NO MORE OUTSIDDERS

MAHI SANGANI

Made with ♥ on the Notion Press Platform
www.notionpress.com

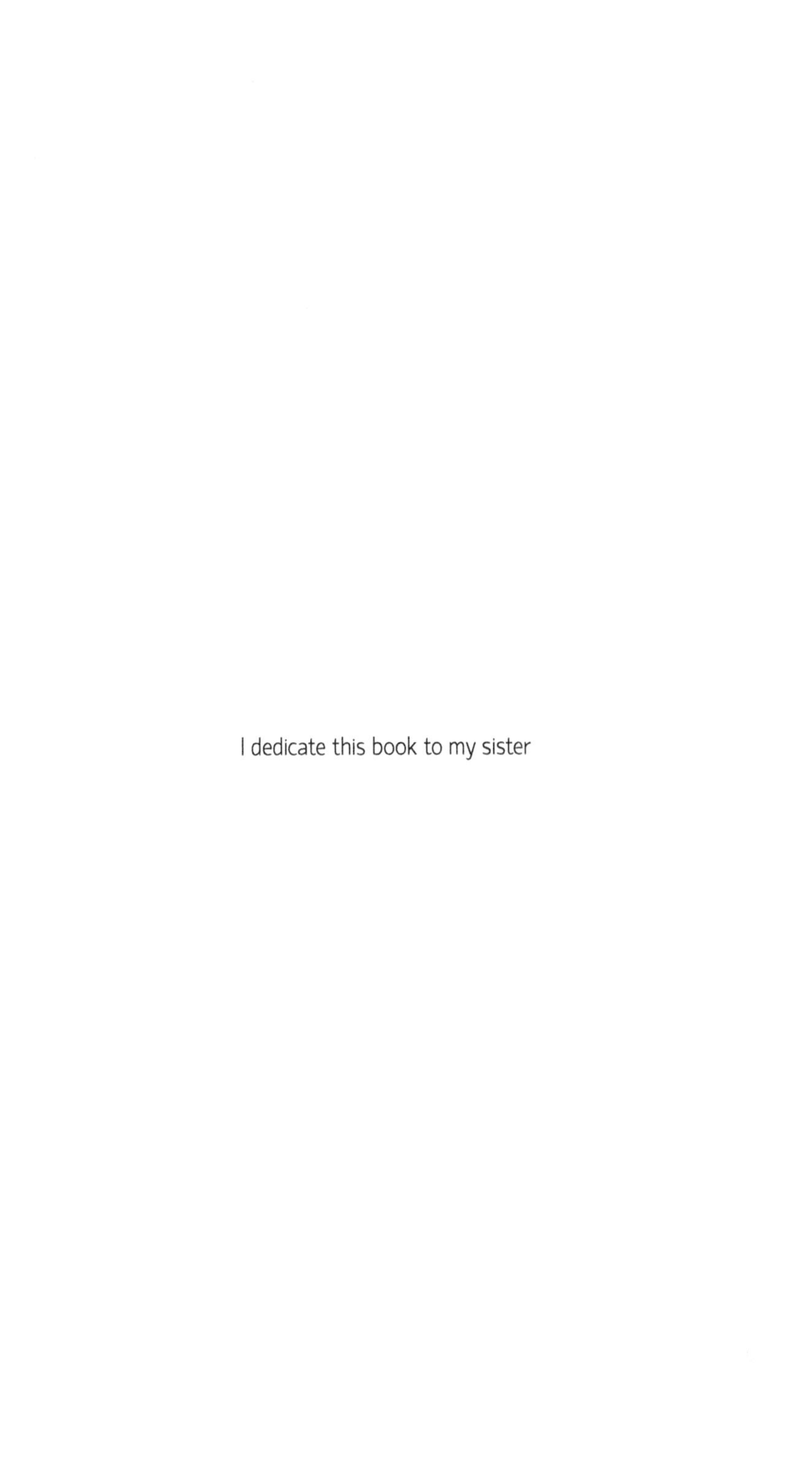

I dedicate this book to my sister

Contents

Early Days

War

Marriage

Truth Revealed

Foreword

I like to write about historical fiction so I came up

Preface

My purpose to come up with this book is I like to write about history and fiction so I came up with this

Acknowledgements

I acknowledge my parents...

CHAPTER ONE

Part-1 Vanshika

As you know this is the story of Vanshika was is the princess of ranthombore by her destiny.

Early days

Vanshika is a girl who was actually born in Amravati, but listed here as a girl they made her sink in water. But the earth was kind, at the same time, The king of ranthambore always wished to get a daughter, He went to the near by river, He found a girl and listed her as the princess of Ranthambore, Her name was Vanshika.....

Years passed,

Vanshika was 10 years old, she always wanted to become a ruler but her second mom was always jealous from her. She once asked her mom can I enter in the battlefield, her mom said, if you have a horse and a practice of sword. Highly influenced Vanshika, went to horse house and asked about a horse, she got a horse and named her Chandravali, learning horse ridding at the this age was highly achievable.

War

VANSHIKA

War days....

The war was caused at haldighati, where there was 20,000 millatry army whereas,Mughals had 2,00,000.

King had already made a defeat by learning the military army, but Vanshika was a streak of light, she said we'll fight. It took 7 days. At final King won the fight. It was a very emotional moment, what he thought and what it happened......

Marriage

VANSHIKA

Marriage

It was her marriage time, but Vanshika always wanted to be a ruler, he asked her husband to be, can I, He said ya sure why not, this was a very happy moment for her, But her mom was not liking this. But her in-laws were very supportive, by this she was known to a very goof female ruler....

Truth revealed

Vanshika came to Ranthombore to give her parents surprise, at that time her mom and dad were taling about her adopted, all thi swas listened by Vanshika, she was very emotional and happy too. She asked her parents is this true, their parents were in shock, but truth has to be revealed one day and it was, they rvealed all the story infront of her. She was happy as from growing to a middle-class family she was to a palace.

She said, whatever happens is best in the life.....